CW01627977

— The Pocket Erotica Series —

Don't Touch
Anne-Gabriel Meusnier de Querlon
Pocket Erotica [№ 1]

A Coming of Age
Jacques Rochette de La Morlière Pocket Erotica [№ 2]

The School of Women
Nicolas Chorier
Pocket Erotica [№ 3]

Priapeia
ed., Lawrence Hamilton
Pocket Erotica [№ 4]

Foot Notes
Restif de la Bretonne
Pocket Erotica [№ 5]

From Their Lips to His Ear
Denis Diderot
Pocket Erotica [№ 6]

Further Studies: The School of Women
Nicolas Chorier
Pocket Erotica [№ 7]

Poems of Lust & Desire
Various
Pocket Erotica [№ 8]

Poems for Her & Odes in Her Honor
Paul Verlaine
Pocket Erotica [№ 9]

Travels to Merryland
Roger Pheuquewell, Esq.
Pocket Erotica [№ 10]

Debauch-O-Rama
John Wilmot
Pocket Erotica [№ 11]

Une galerie d'érotisme
Various
Pocket Erotica [№ 12]

Eve's Academy
Eurydice
Pocket Erotica [№ 13]

A Dirty Story as You Like It
Kim Vodicka
Pocket Erotica [№ 14]

A Good Girl's Home Companion
Anonymous
Pocket Erotica [№ 15]

Retaliation
Marquis de Sade
Pocket Erotica [№ 17]

Jancy Quixote
Doug Rice
Pocket Erotica [№ 18]

Escape Artists
Su Orwell
Pocket Erotica [№ 19]

The Self-Made Cuckold
Marquis de Sade
Pocket Erotica [№ 20]

Selected Erotic Poems
Charles Baudelaire
Pocket Erotica [№ 21]

Jean-Fucque
Louis Aragon, R J Dent
Pocket Erotica [№ 22]

A Handbook of Manners for the Good Girls of France
Pierre Louÿs
Pocket Erotica [№ 23]

The Duped Judge
Marquis de Sade
Pocket Erotica [№ 24]

The Obedience Room
Catherine D'Avis
Pocket Erotica [№ 25]

The Desire Box
Laure Favager
Pocket Erotica [№ 26]

Grand Hotel Vittoria
Nina Ansani
Pocket Erotica [№ 27]

A Filthly Letter
Théophile Gautier
Pocket Erotica [№ 28]

Sin & Other Stories
Andreia Rodrigues
Pocket Erotica [№ 29]

Sin

& Other Stories

Andreia Rodrigues

POCKET EROTICA #29

Copyright © 2024 by Andreia Rodrigues

Pocket Erotica
(№ 29)

All Rights Reserved.

ISBN 979-8-9908521-7-4

Cover photograph: Brian Lawson

NEW URGE EDITIONS
an imprint of Black Scat Books
BlackScatBooks.com

Contents

SIN 7

RELEASE 25

THE CANAL 53

SIN

EMILY RETRIEVED THE NOTEBOOK from her backpack, pressed it against her lap, under the desk. It was History class, they sat in groups of five. She looked above her shoulders, the teacher had his face buried in a book, his cigar forming white paths above his head. She turned to Tara, by her side, with nostrils enlarged.

"You wanna see it?" Emily whispered.

"Uh-huh," said Tara.

"Keep it on your lap, okay?"

"Okay."

Emily placed the notebook on Tara's

lap. Tara's thighs trembled, she glanced at the teacher. His eyes remained cast down.

"Girls," Tara muttered to the other girls at the table. Four pairs of wide eyes fixed on her. "Please cover my view. Lean on the table so no one sees me." They all leaned forward, a mix of fear and titillation etching into their faces.

Tara opened the notebook in the middle. The images, although they met her eyes for only a few seconds, would imprint in her mind like a tattoo.

A woman, naked. Entirely. She was on her knees, on a bed of white sheets, legs apart. Her breasts, ripe like melons, pointing forwards – plentiful, sovereign. Tara's glance trailed the woman's tiny waist until her hair-free vulva. Oh! Between the woman's legs, right there on the pinkish flesh, the head of a man lay, his tongue tucked in the middle of her labia. The woman's head was reared back, eyes half-closed, mouth wet and open – the howl of pleasure about to escape the page.

Tara's breathing got cut. Blood flew through her with a new rhythm, a new urgency, a new warmth. Her full body in heat. Her sex pulsed. She pressed her legs tight.

"Let me see, let me see." Kelly, by her side, reached for the notebook.

Tara held it back. "No, just let me finish."

On the next page, the same woman, blond curls hovering above her head, still that half-fainted expression frozen on her face. She stood on the deck of a ship, legs wide open. A man sat under her, face docked in the center, his tongue parting the bloated lips of her vulva. Her labia were even more swollen and viscous than in the previous picture, the tongue, thicker. The woman's hands grabbed the grids, so as not to dissolve with pleasure. At the bottom of the page, there was a close-up image of the curl of the man's tongue folding the clitoris.

Blood left Tara's head. She thought she would faint.

"My turn." Kelly grabbed the notebook from her hands.

Air came back to Tara's lungs. She breathed fast. All her nerves opened, craving climax. Desire traversed her body like lava.

In her eighteen years, Tara had never seen a porn magazine. As fervent Catholics, her parents had built an invisible wall to protect their daughters against the sins of the flesh. Regulars at the local church, were one of the few families who strictly followed the Ten Commandments. No sensual scenes were allowed near their home, not even the French kisses from the afternoon *telenovelas*. The "s" word was a damnation, not to be spoken about. Even though Tara possessed some understanding of the scientific account of sex and reproduction – provided by the public schools – it had never sunk into her the materialization of a woman undressing herself *fully* for a man. Of a woman shaving her sex and stretching it wide, in front of a male's face. Let alone a man tucking his tongue down there, sucking it, tasting it. The overload of sensations arising from the pictures was tremendous.

It was shocking, frightening. It was electrifying.

The notebook passed lap by lap underneath the table and returned to Emily's backpack. The four girls got all flushed, gasping, their thighs pressing hard.

"Oh, my," Kelly said. "Does your brother have more of these things?"

"Yep. Loads. But this is the one I like the most." Emily smirked. Her familiarity with the content made her more in control of her desire.

"Let us see again," said Tiffany.

Emily shook her head. "It's too dangerous, you girls are all red on your faces. The teacher is not stupid. Maybe later you can see it again."

Tara never saw the photos again. She didn't need to. They engraved in her mind, in vivid colors.

Her body experienced a new kind of hunger and restlessness for the remainder of the school day. The pinkish flesh of tongue and labia fondling, ecstasy distorting the woman's features – images clung in the air like a presence.

At home, her mother was by the kitchen sink seasoning a chicken. "How did the geography test go?"

Ah, that's right. Tara had taken a Geography test; it had been before the magazine. She had no memory of it. "It was okay, Mum."

"You okay?" Her Mum frowned.

"Uh-huh. Why?"

"You seem a little pale."

"I have a headache. I'll try to take a nap."

Her mum's eyebrows raised. "Nap?

You never take naps."

"I might have one today. I'll try."

"Tell me if you need a pill for the headache. And ah, don't forget to study for church school."

Oh yeah, that stupid biblical test. Tara was going to be christened soon and would have to pass an exam. "I won't, Mum."

Tara hated church school. First, she was the oldest there. Due to her big sister's leukaemia, Tara had dropped most activities, she even missed a school year. Second, as much as she tried, deep inside she never cared much about the five venial sins and things like that. Sure, she prayed with gratitude for God to have cured her sister, but all the rigidity of the church made her cringe.

On that afternoon after school, Tara

locked the door of her bedroom soundlessly – locked doors were forbidden. She took the porcelain of Our Lady of Lourdes – a gift from her grandmother – out of sight; buried it inside a drawer. She pulled out her panties. The cotton was glistening wet.

On the bed, she spread her legs open. She had never dared to do that before. She had felt the urge to rub herself on the edge of the mattress, sometimes on the pillow, but always with her underwear on. Now, what a delight, the feeling of her exposed sex wide open, misty air caressing it. Oh, that's why the blond woman did it. It was so good. Imagine it could get even better? She pictured a tongue scrolling down there, retracting and pressing, retracting and pressing. Moistness spread to her thighs.

She wouldn't dare to touch herself. But blind with desire, she frenzied to do something, anything. She lingered at the end of the bed and rubbed the naked flesh against the edge of the mattress. Mmm... The contact of the delicate skin with the hard fabric deprived her of her senses. Lightning flashes of ecstasy traversed her body, the insides of her thighs quivered. She stroked more, her hips rolling over and over. She was out of her mind; she would not have stopped for anything in the world. Even if someone knocked on the door, even if the ceiling fell on her head. She would keep stroking in circles, her sex drooling on the soft sheets, staining them wet.

An explosion inside of her. A self-dissolving orgasmic bliss. She buried her mouth in a pillow to muffle a cry. Her heart attempted to leave her chest; air turned dense. Her legs lost their strength, her body collapsed on the bed.

Oh, boy. What was that? She had never reached that point. Her prior rubbing adventures had ended with her legs growing tired, desire still pulsing her sex. But that – it was violent, convulsive, dizzying. It was marvelous.

Fever slowly evaporated from her body; her veins calmed. Consciousness returned.

Oh, Lord. What had she done? So nasty, so sinful. Guilt grabbed her by the neck.

How was she going to appear at the church now? Her christening! Before the ceremony, she would have to confess to the priest. To tell her sins, or else she wouldn't receive the Ostia. Holly mother of God. Her body was no longer worthy of receiving Christ's soul. How would she explain to her parents that she could no longer be christened?

Regret clouded over Tara the entire day after. By the afternoon, she calmed. It had just been one time, if she never did it again, maybe God would forgive her. She would kneel on corn and pray a hundred Our Fathers and a hundred Holy Mary's.

But at night, in the dark, she forgot all of that. The pages of the magazine would unveil in front of her eyes, charging her body with desire. Unable to fight, she surrendered. She explored new areas: pinched her nipples, leafed through her labia, dipped her fingers in the moisture. Spread the vulva open with two fingers, glided the fingers up and down like a brush on canvas. She poked the little hard dot on the top. Mmm. The biggest shivers reverberated from there.

Sometimes she would orgasm more than twice, and swallow bitter guilt right after.

Purple circles started forming around Tara's eyes. Remorse mixed with maddening pleasure and consumed her.

"Are you on a diet?" her mum asked.

"No."

"You don't have to be thinner to fit your christening dress, you know."

"I'm not on a diet, Mum. I'm just not so hungry these days, that's all."

Last church school day before confession. Tara no longer looked the teacher in the eye.

"I have an announcement for you,

class." The teacher ambled across the classroom, hands to the back.

Oh, no. Could he know? The teacher was a priest apprentice, these people were said to receive messages from God. Had God told him what Tara did between her bedsheets?

The teacher cleared his throat. "You're no longer having the traditional confession with the priest. You're going to have a collective self-confession." The word *collective* raised Tara's hairs. The teacher rubbed his cassock. "It will go like this: all of you will think of your sins, imagine you're bringing them out of you and depositing them in your hands. Then you will walk to the altar, carry your sins with you and leave them in a blessed vessel. Then you'll promise not to commit those sins again. You'll pray twenty Our-

Fathers and like this, and you'll be ready to receive the Ostia."

The class exhaled; Tara's shoulder fell with relief. That was the best news of the year. She wouldn't have to verbalize her lust to a representative of God.

As the self-confession idea freed Tara, her erotic sessions grew wilder. She experimented with other tactile sensations: a feather, the edges of a pillow, the corner of a desk, the current of the shower pointed straight there. On the bed, naked, she threw her legs in the air, pictured a dozen tongues on her. One at each nipple, a large one on the vulva, others around her thighs. She adventured a finger inside, from where the honey flowed.

She signed a pact with herself: she would bathe in pleasure, get smeared with her own nectar, until confession day. She would then self-confess, in silence, imagining her sins falling into her hands. She would walk down the altar, throw them there and leave, clean. Five Our Fathers later she would be free, and start a new life, without sins.

On confession day, her eyes filled with tears. The shame and the perspective of never rubbing herself again: which one was more dreadful she couldn't tell. Yet, she deposited her sins on the blessed vessel and promised to stop committing them.

At the christening ceremony, she received the Ostia with a sense of cleanliness. She had sinned, but she regretted it and would start a new chapter with God.

"Congratulations, darling."

Her dad's eyes shone. "I'm proud of you," he said, touching the sleeve of her white dress. She was his sweet little girl. Innocent, pure.

That evening, she left the lights in her bedroom on during the night. When desire crawled between her legs like ants, she sprayed cold water on her face.

Her stoic resistance succeeded for a week. On the seventh day, desire poured, from every pore. She undressed in one move, as if possessed, abandoning her flesh to the most maddening forms of pleasure she could elicit.

The images from the porn magazine hunted Tara for decades. They dragged her to public restrooms – in restaurants, trains, workplace – to appease the fever with her fingers. Once a mature woman, the images would evoke guilt-free joy.

However, another form of pain replaced guilt – the sorrow of never being in the place of the blond woman. Of never encountering a man who would tuck his head between her legs, roll his tongue smoothly, taste her with so much eagerness, that her head would fall, and her mouth would open for a howl of pleasure.

RELEASE

LAURA POSED A HAND over her eyes to block the bright noon sun. The rest of the apple she failed to finish was half covered by ants under the bench. By her side, Teresa stared at a couple making out by the trunk of a Jacaranda tree. Laura followed her friend's gaze. Below the purple crown of flowers cascading from the tree, the man had his hands full with the woman's face, their tongues intertwined like snakes.

"Fourteen months, Teresa," Laura said. "Fourteen months it has been since I've been like that with someone."

Teresa grinned. "At least you aren't risking getting pregnant."

Laura sighed, her gaze lost in the distance. "I'm starting to find myself imagining how random men look like naked."

"Oh, dear." Teresa chuckled. "I know what you mean. But if you insist on not using Tinder things become difficult."

"Argh. I'm tired of the hookups we get on Tinder. All that bullshit of guys treating us like a piece of cheap meat. Or the other bullshit of holding yourself back, not showing too much interest, to not scare nice guys away. Or worse — shaving yourself completely before a bad date that leads to nothing."

Teresa shook her head. "Tell me about it."

"I miss a man's sweaty body against

mine." Laura laid a hand on her breastbone, lowered her voice. "I miss dick. But to be honest, I hate the work sex gives. I hate that I need to make my sex smell of coconut and look like a rose."

Teresa laughed more, crossed her ankles. "Yep. Porn has ruined things for us."

"Exactly. Not that the past was better for women, but at least men in the 80s had no problem with natural bodies. Not with pubic hair, at least."

"Uh-huh." Teresa narrowed her eyes. "I remember my uncle's old magazines. I once found them in his basement. Pubic hair all over the pages."

Laura pursed her lips. A ray of sunshine highlighted the copper color of her hair. "Oh, can you imagine a man who wouldn't give a damn and just go down there, lick with hair and everything? Delight himself and didn't care. Stick his face there as if sucking from a mango."

Laura and Teresa sighed and crossed their legs, their cheeks flushed.

"This reminds me of the most arousing talk I've ever heard," said Teresa. "You know that guy…Marcelo. I think that's his name. Also a postgrad. History class, brown beard, long hair in a ponytail?"

"Yeah, I've seen him. Kind of attractive."

"He sure is. Once on the bus, I sat in front of him and his friends. You can't believe what they were saying." Teresa leaned to face Laura, shaking her ponytail over her shoulders. "The bus was quite empty. I don't think they thought I could hear them. Anyway. Marcelo, or whatever his name is, was saying, 'Boy, I love pussy. I mean, all of them.' Then someone said, 'Who doesn't?' and Marcelo said, 'No man, I mean I *really* love pussies. I love their smell; I love their taste.'"

Laura's heartbeat quickened. "Oh, my."

"Uh-huh. He also said, 'I love licking pussy, man. I could do that all day. To feel them getting wet in my mouth.'"

"Oh, Teresa." Laura adjusted her hips on the bench. "I'm getting aroused."

"I know! I needed a finger job just thinking about it." Teresa fanned her face. "But that wasn't all. His friends all talked at once, I didn't quite understand what came next, but at some point, I heard him saying, 'You know guys, I like it so much that if I had to choose between never licking a pussy again or never having a blow job, I would choose the latter."

Laura's breathing grew faster. She looked away, swallowed. A milky liquid moistened her underwear.

Teresa smirked. "Amazing, isn't it?"

"Oh, dear." Laura bit her lip.

"Ah! I forgot the best part." Teresa jumped. "At some point in their talk, someone else said something like, 'I like it too, but it has to be a very clean pussy, you know,' to what Marcelo said, 'Sure, a clean one. But just clean enough. I don't like pussy with the taste of roses. I like pussy tasting of pussy.'"

Laura pressed her legs together and gasped. "Really? Did he say that?"

"Yep." Teresa passed her tongue over her lips.

"Do you know if he is single?"

Teresa cocked her head to the side. "I think he is. He is on Tinder, anyway."

"Why haven't you contacted him yet?" Laura almost shouted.

"I'm waiting on that fool, Carli. I really like that idiot."

"Oh, boy. I don't think Carli will be any better than this Marcelo guy seems to be."

Back in class, Laura didn't listen to a word the International Relations teacher said. Her lower belly burned with desire. No matter how important the content of the class was for the exam, she would not let go of the sensual thoughts. Tongues on her flesh, fingers parting the lips of her sex. Oh, how soothing that lascivious heat, running through her veins. It overpowered anything on the way – fear, loss, regret.

Once at home, Laura headed straight to her bedroom.

"Aren't you having dinner?" her mum asked. "I made tacos."

"Not yet, I have migraines."

Laura closed the curtains and threw off her clothes. On the bed, her legs parted. Cold air blew softly at her swollen vulva. Marcelo entered her mind. The tip of his tongue out, thirsty for her. The tongue laid on her nipples, making circles, living wet marks. Her nipples puffed up, hardened at the tip of her fingers. Her legs parted wider still, her fingers slid down, the way Marcelo's tongue would. Gently, then firm, his beard covered with the nectar of her. The creamy noise of the moisture leaking from her sex filled the room. Just three finger rounds and she collapsed to the side, ecstasy shivering from underneath her skin.

Still breathing heavily, she reached for her laptop. The list of History students on the department web page was easy to find. Marcelo Arantes, third-year student, major in Contemporary Territorial Conflicts. In his profile picture, he threw a mild smile, sprinkled with irony. If one stared long enough at the depths of his hazelnut eyes, hunger would be found.

It did not take much to locate him on Facebook either. Great, Laura didn't have to re-open her Tinder account.

Her friend request was accepted within minutes. She quickly clicked on Messenger.

Hi Marcelo. I guess you don't know me.

I'm in Political Science, second year. I've seen you on campus and felt like getting in touch. I'd love to get to know you better.

Straight to the point. No preambles, no aloofness, no bullshit. Laura didn't use to be like that. But lately, life had thrown enough at her face for her to care. The stroke of her father. The painful break-up of a six-year relationship with her high school sweetheart. He had cheated on her with his own cousin. Seriously? Sure, she had the biggest breasts of the whole town, but of all women…

Laura was too disappointed with life, and let's face it – she thought — too horny to care.

The answer on Messenger came right away, with reciprocal directedness.

Hi, darling. Such a delight to receive

your message. I've seen you on campus and would love to take you out.

Perfect. No walking around in circles.

A dozen messages later, the date was settled. For Friday, three days from now.

At the university park the next day, Teresa's jaw dropped.

"I can't believe you're going for it." A smile took over her face. "Well done, girl. Next week, I want to hear everything. *Everything*."

Laura crossed her arms. "I hope he means what he said to his friends on the bus, you know." She paused and giggled. "But if not, it's about time to get laid again."

What a relief to not have crossed Marcelo on campus that day. Audacity revealed itself much easier behind a screen than in physical presence.

In the late afternoon, she sat in her bedroom, writing an essay when the phone vibrated. A message popped on the screen.

Hi, darling. Hope you had a good day. I'm looking forward to Friday.

Me too. After a pause she added, *Did you think about a nice place to go?*

He replied within seconds. *I was thinking, why don't you come to my house first, and from here we'll decide together where to go?*

Hmm. He seemed to be in the same hastiness as she. *Sounds like a good plan. I'll be there. See you Friday.*

See you, darling. Just one more thing. Don't worry about preparing yourself too much for our date. I like a natural woman.

Interesting. Where was Marcelo going with that? Wherever it was, Laura felt released from constraints.

Oh, yeah? Do you want me all natural for you? I like that.

There was no hesitation in his reply. *Yeah, babe. I want to kiss you all over. As you are. If you let me, of course.*

On her bed, Laura leaned against the pillow. A voluptuous feeling ran over her body. This man wasn't fooling around. Another message followed.

Sorry, darling. I crossed a line here, didn't I? I apologize. I didn't mean to be a jerk.

A smile lifted her cheeks.

Don't worry. I think we both want the same thing here.

She held her breath and thought of something naughty to type. What the hell? Let's just send it.

You're getting me wet.

A few seconds went by, and blood pulsed at her temples. Before regret materialized within her, new words appeared on the screen:

Hmmm. I'm hard for you, girl. I'm going to kiss you like you have never been kissed before. And I don't only mean your mouth.

Desire traversed her like fire.

You're driving me crazy, Marcelo. I have to go now to appease myself.

Oh, darling. Don't! Save it all for me. Why don't you come to my place now?

With that, Laura went for a shower. When she passed the soap between her legs, ecstasy nearly took over. Her hand withdrew just in time.

She dressed in the only brand-new lingerie she had: a white brasserie matching lace panties. The light color emphasized her caramel skin, the delicate fabric settled like a bow wrapping a gift.

She ambled towards the door when her mum shouted from the kitchen.

"Don't be late. Your father has to go to the doctor tomorrow. I'll shower him this evening and I need your help to lift him from the bed." Her mum, always with that imperishable face of hers — a face whose features were like acrylic; nothing could shatter them.

"Okay, I'll be back by nine o'clock."

Laura would never forget that one afternoon, a year ago, when they received the phone call from her father's job. They had never called before. Something had happened; her father was at the hospital.

The stroke paralyzed half his body. His intellect and speech were affected too. Nothing in Laura's twenty-five years of life had hurt as much as watching her dad go from an active tree surgeon to someone confined to a bed, who didn't seem to remember who she was. In a year, she circled through denial, anger, and acceptance. Still, there were plenty of nights when she cried herself to sleep.

But on the way to Marcelo's flat, the struggles of everyday life seemed unreal. His messages hovered in her mind, warming the bottom of her belly and making her nipples tingle. The anticipation of that feeling of sweet abandon that only sex brings lifted her spirits.

Apartment seventy-two, fifth floor on the student housing private flats. Upon two knocks, the door opened.

"Hi, darling. So glad you came."

How sweet that he said 'darling' a lot.

His ponytail was undone. The water dropping from his curls formed a dark stain on his t-shirt. Up close, his features looked more mature, although softer than from a distance.

A couch the size of a pool table, a TV set and a bookshelf composed the living area. Red curtains blocked the outside view.

Marcelo threw a penetrating smile. His eyes carried the depths of a night of incongruent dreams. In the center of the room, he grabbed Laura's waist, gently but firmly, and breathed out a warm desire. His lips tasted of mint. She answered to his tongue with equal hunger, squeezing the muscles of his back. His fingers slid under her dress, gripping her butt with both hands and rubbing her body against his stiff sex.

His tongue moved from her lips to the lobe of her ear.

“Look at the state you put me in,” he whispered.

“I see.” Laura gasped. “We’re going to have some fun.”

“You betcha.”

With his lips on hers, Marcelo guided their entwined bodies to the couch. He laid her down as an experienced waiter serving a banquet. She leaned on a pillow and spread her legs. Her dress loosened down, revealing the delicate panties glistening with wetness. He drew her panties off and held them between his fingers. “Hmm. Look at this,” he murmured, licking the moisture on the fabric, eyes closed as he savored the sensation. Laura’s inner thighs shivered, and she let out a gasp. In response, he knelt down.

"Let's see what we have here," he whispered, feasting his eyes on the glowing skin. Her sex was dark-pink and turgid, a fine layer of hair forming a gracious curtain on the sides. He leaned in and sniffed between her legs.

"Mmm. Open a little more for me, love. Open." Marcelo whispered. Laura complied, and a silky moisture started forming a circle on the couch.

"Mmm. She likes me, doesn't she?" Marcelo murmured, his voice thick with desire.

"Uh-huh." Laura gasped in response, her breath hitching.

Marcelo gently opened her sex like a bud. With two fingers running down, he sent shivers all over her body. Up and down, up and down, the tip of his fingers slid easily over her sensitive skin.

"So beautiful," Marcelo whispered, admiring the intimate sight before him. He carefully opened the two little lips of her vulva more, revealing the red-rose layers underneath.

"Ahh," Laura moaned softly, bringing her arms to her thighs, increasing the distance between them.

"You want me, don't you?" Marcelo asked, his voice husky with desire.

"Uh-huh," Laura breathed heavily, her anticipation palpable.

"I'll give what you want. But first, I'm gonna kiss her, like I've never kissed any other pussy before."

The tip of his tongue darted at her clitoris, swept back and forth.

"Ohh..."

He then buried his whole face

between her parted legs, and engulphed her sex with voracious kisses, as if kissing her mouth. His tongue stroking her swollen lips, almost depriving Laura of her senses.

"Ahh, ahh..."

"Come on my mouth, love, come."

Laura's spine curled. No other pleasure she had ever felt, equated to that. Complete surrender. No intrusive thoughts of shame, no concerns. Her legs spread out to ecstasy, her toes curling.

Pleasure became so immense, that she howled, "Aaaah."

Laura's legs collapsed on the bed.

Marcelo stood up. Caressed her rosy cheeks, her parted lips. She licked and sucked his fingers.

"I want you," she whispered.

He drew her dress up over her head,

freed her brasserie. Two small, firm breasts pointed at him. He licked the tips of his fingers and made circles around the nipples.

"Mmmm."

His pants went down, and before she could think, he had a condom in his hands. A beautiful rigid sex he had, impeccable as polished dark marble. It slipped easily inside her. So wet was she, that the noise of hands slapping water filled the room.

His whole weight upon her, he whispered against her ear, "I'm gonna stay inside you all night long."

Laura didn't hold her cries of pleasure. "Ahhhhh…"

Marcelo's moves got faster, drops of sweat fell from his forehead to her breasts. She spread the moist dropping off his skin around her nipples with the tip of her fingers. He moaned loudly and half-fainted by her side.

Marcelo took Laura in his arms, her head resting on his chest where his heartbeat pounded like the rhythm of a galloping horse. Outside, the distant cheers from a football field mingled with the calls of kingbirds.

From the couch, Laura glanced at the titles on his bookshelf: *One Hundred Years of Solitude*, *The Shadow of the Wind*, *Biography of Che Guevara*, *Pluralism in Ecosystem Governance*. She wanted to ask if he had read them all, but a delightful languor held her. He ran his fingers through her hair as she kissed his chest, which still faintly smelled of shampoo.

"Was it good, darling?" His voice had

acquired a husky, dreamy tone.

"That was amazing," she replied.

"*You* are amazing." He glided the tip of his fingers around her back, tracing the contours of her spine.

"You really like a woman's body, don't you?"

"Yeah. Since the first time I saw a woman naked, I got fanatic about the female body."

Laura grinned. "When was this? The first sight of a naked woman?"

"Long ago. From a magazine, of course. My big brother's *Playboys*." He sighed. "The sight of pussy...There's nothing like that." He paused, searching for words. "It's like... It's like a crack, a rupture on the skin. But skillfully done. As if someone stopped midway in carving himself to paradise."

Marcelo's words deepened Laura's fascination and torpor. She tried to speak but just a gasp came out. She shivered as his fingers travelled down to the valley between her legs, from behind. She opened the way slightly. Before surrendering further to pleasure, a thought crossed her mind.

"So, you have a brother." She lifted her chin. "How is he? I mean, does he look like you?"

Marcelo chuckled. "Are you interested in my brother too?"

Laura flushed. "No. I just wanted to know more about you, that's all."

He touched her cheeks as if to dispel the fresh pinkness and gently guided her head back to his chest. "Sorry, I didn't mean it in a bad way. But about me, my life, there's nothing that interesting, really. My brother moved to Europe with his wife. Somewhere in Spain."

"How about your parents?"

Marcelo cleared his throat. "My mother ran away when I was five years old. I barely remember her. My father never stopped drinking ever since."

Laura looked into his eyes. Tenderness emanated from them.

"I'm sorry to hear that," she said, and kissed his eyelids.

He bit her lower lip. "Don't be. As long as I have a delicious woman by my side, I'm happy."

He went down on her. Caressed her pubic hair, his tongue making its way between the lips of her vulva. "I can do this all day if you let me."

Honey poured from her.

At 8:45 pm, Laura left Marcelo's flat,

her legs weak from an overdose of pleasure. What started that evening evolved into a casual yet long-term relationship. In the initial weeks, they spent nearly every other evening together. Her phone buzzed throughout the day with messages from him.

I'm thinking of that hot pussy of yours. I wish I could kiss her right here, on the train.

I still have her smell on my beard. It's driving me crazy.

Is she wet? Tell me she's wet.

To what Laura would answer: *Yes, she is so wet that my pants are getting moist. All I can think is to open my legs wide for you.*

One time, when he went on a two-week trip with his friends, he wrote: *Don't shave her. I want her wild. I want to groom her like the beautiful naughty pussy she is.*

He would apply Laura's lip gloss on

her sex, and brush rouge over it. Once he asked her to keep her unwashed underwear: *Wear it all day and bring it to me. I want to have the smell of your body. Strong female smell. Delicious pussy scent.*

Oh, Marcelo. He gave Laura the best year of her life, despite her struggles with passing Political Philosophy or Public Law by the end of the term. Even amidst her family's challenges in finding healthcare for her father, the significance of everything seemed to blur whenever Marcelo went down and kissed her sex as he would kiss her mouth.

THE CANAL

"WE'RE SORRY, VANESSA," SAID the manager from across the table—the damn table where Vanessa was used to delivering piles of reports. Some of the dossiers, she had typed late at night, including weekends. Typing the night away, one cup of unsweetened coffee after another. Sometimes cold coffee, even. All that for what? Her efforts had failed to prevent the worst.

The manager coughed. "It's painful to fire you, and I mean it. But with the pandemic, our sales decreased drastically. There's not much we can do at this moment."

Vanessa pressed her lips. Tears were gathering behind her eyelids. The manager's moustache bounced. "I'll write a good reference for you," he said, rubbing the bald top of his head.

Outside, the sky was dark grey in her honor, mirroring the shades of her defeat. Vanessa envied everyone she crossed on the streets. The waiters taking orders on the terraces, the police officers, the mailman, the bus driver. All of them had a job.

Where else would she find an assistant sales manager position without a master's degree? She had experience, sure, but that wasn't enough nowadays. That job at Clerk & Carl Associates had been an arrangement between her brother and his best friend in college over a decade ago.

The option of going back to university was dreary. She would have to apply for a mature student scholarship, such a lean studentship that would require her to move to a student house. Oh, Lord. Sharing a bathroom! There was no worse nightmare for a woman in her thirties. Dealing with youngsters' hormones, dirt, and hangovers—she had passed the age for that.

On that evening, back from the last day at the company, the entrance of her building acquired a new allure. How hadn't she noticed the climbing plants ornamenting the cracks in the walls? The faded-red tiles on the floor, bringing memories of childhood? The smell of baked cookies wafting from the ground-floor neighbor's window?

Oh, the cozy smell of her apartment, a mix of old books and sandalwood. She already missed the place's noises and contours. The joyful cheer of drunk people wandering down the pavement on Saturday night. The ear-scratch sex moans of her lascivious neighbor, making her feel like a lonely loser, but reminding her that, despite pain and loss, there was pleasure in the world.

Even if Vanessa decided not to return to college, she would have to find an apartment outside the center. Unemployment support wouldn't allow her to pay for such a nice place where everything was within a twenty-minute reach.

She drank the half bottle of white wine that had been resting inside the fridge for over a month. She fell asleep before twilight. Yet, in the early morning, Vanessa's head pounded with the headache of a sleepless night out. From behind the curtains of her bedroom, the sun was shining gold. How did it dare?

The hot shower brought some comfort, like warm hands over her shoulders. Hot green tea cleared her head—everyone in Toulouse seemed to be adhering to some Japanese tradition.

At the kitchen table, the silence of Sunday screamed inside her ears. The ticks of the clock above the sink appeared to grow louder, taking over the entire house. She started doing the dishes but quit halfway. Unable to bring herself to do anything useful, Vanessa put on her walking shoes and left for the only place that calmed her senses—the canal.

How many times had she walked

from beginning to end, a two-hour-long endeavor? But it never felt too long. The sensorial delight was soothing—the rustle of the leaves, the cries of the birds, the shades of the passers-by reflecting the waveless current. The boats lingering, unhurried, carrying people and their floating homes. Homes over water. She imagined the people living there, drinking tea, cooking, sleeping. Making love.

There was a favorite boat she looked forward to approaching. Nothing special about the boat, the appeal set on its owner. A man with long limbs and solid muscles often stood outside. Sometimes he was cleaning, making repairs. Other times he was drinking coffee by the canal, a book in his hand. With his Ray-Ban glasses, he looked like someone who could solve a Rubik's cube.

"Afternoon," he would say and exhibit a charmingly shy grin.

Vanessa would retribute the smile and continue her path, wishing that his glance was laying on her *derrière*, admiring the undulations her flesh drew from underneath the skirt. Further along the canal, she would be caught by the mental images her mind created of him. His heavy body lying on a low bed, legs apart, gazing at the river by his window. Reading a book, Sartre perhaps, while the river breeze blew underneath his shorts.

That day, Vanessa spotted the man from afar. He was cleaning the windows of his boat, shirtless. The sun imprinted on his bronze skin. The sudden ardor crawling between her legs surprised

Vanessa. Desire contracted her lower belly like a tight belt.

The closer she got the more succulent the man's skin looked. The muscles of his back contracted in voluptuous shapes. By the time she crossed him, her cheeks were red hot.

"Afternoon," he said and adjusted his glasses up his nose.

"Afternoon." It took a few seconds for her to notice she had stopped walking, her eyes fixed on the sweat drops above his forehead. She cleared her throat. "You seem to have a lot of work to do here."

The man dropped the sponge he was holding in a bucket. His smile grew. "Not much more, no. Just one more window."

What a great effort not to stare at his chest. From closer, he was less muscled than she had marveled. Yet, his torso ha a firmness languidly contrasted by soft contours. How good would it be to bite his flesh, she thought.

"Good luck with the cleaning," Vanessa said and managed to bring her legs to move.

"Thank you." She had advanced a few steps when he added, "I'm Hector, by the way."

She turned. "Nice to meet you, Hector. I'm Vanessa."

"Glad to finally meet you. You come here often, don't you?" He moved his glasses up his nose again. Why did that gesture cause her heart to speed?

"Yep. Every time the weather is good I come here for a walk."

Hector hid his hands inside his pockets.

"It must be nice to have a boat," Vanessa said, moving closer to him.

"It sure is. But it's a lot of work, you know."

"I can imagine. Don't you have anyone with you…I mean, to help."

"Nope. I'm all alone." He gazed straight into her eyes for the first time.

"Oh, I see." She tossed her hair back. "Is it big enough for you to feel comfortable living there?"

"Uh-huh. Of course, it's not huge, but I'm used to it."

"Nice." Vanessa glanced around. A couple were walking with a dog a few meters away. "I guess I'll continue my walk, before it gets dark."

"Enjoy."

Vanessa waved, "See you, Hector."

"See you, Vanessa."

Did he blink? She couldn't tell for sure.

For the remainder of the walk Vanessa failed in contemplating the rhythms of the river and the chatter of the birds. Her mind stayed with Hector and his boat. The shine on his skin, the messiness of his curly hair. The lyricism of how he moved his glasses up his nose.

On the way back she shivered with expectation of encountering him again. She rushed. Her chest pounded at the sight of him, by the grass with a mug in his hands.

"Hey. You walk quite fast." His face opened to a big smile.

She hid a strand of hair behind an ear. "Yep, I'm a good walker, I think."

"Good you managed before dark."

"Uh-huh, that was the plan."

She was starting to move again when he cleared his throat. His voice a pitch lower. "Would you like to have a look at my boat?" He rubbed his thighs. "I mean, I guess you haven't seen one before, from the inside. Have you?"

Vanessa trembled. After a pause, she said, "No, and I'd love to."

He entered first, held her hand for her to jump inside. The touch of his fingers sent a current over her arms. She tottered; he caught her before she stumbled. "It's a bit tricky, but I have you," he said, beaming, their shoulders touching. He scented of aftershave.

"Look how cute." The kitchen resembled the one of a doll's house, with small, ruffled curtains. Pin-up girl posters hang above the sink.

"It's not so bad," said Hector. "I got it

from my grandparents."

"Lucky you." The coziness of the place relaxed Vanessa's every muscle. She felt walled off from the world.

"That's mostly it." Hector rambled until the end of the kitchen and turned. "Over here is the bedroom. Just two rooms, but I don't need more."

Vanessa followed. A low bed occupied the space. From a pigeon-hole window, the river flew, serene. Shelves with books of all thicknesses loaded the walls below the arms-reach ceiling.

"I see you like to read." Vanessa sat on the edge of the bed, gazing at the books. Something about Hector, about that little home over water, about the way it bounced, brought her into a state of drunkenness. A feeling of openness to the surprises of life, of abandon.

Hector's eyes sparkled as he leaned by the door. "Yep. I like reading. Philosophy and Sociology most."

"Yeah?" Vanessa stretched until her thighs rested on the bed. She puffed her chest up, hands spread on the mattress. Desire etched into her features. "Which philosophers do you read?"

"Sartre, Marx, De Beauvoir..." He lost his words. His glance, fixed at Vanessa's thighs denounced his hunger. She leaned back and pushed her knees open. The hem of the skirt slid up revealing the milky skin.

He lingered towards the bed, his gaze deep into her eyes. Knees on the bed, he paused, waiting for a sign from her. She ran her tongue over her lips, parted her legs more, revealing her underwear – a trail of wetness traversing it.

He gasped. With two fingers, he caressed the moist fabric, pressing hard and soft. Soft and hard, her vulva growing stiff under his touch. "Ahhh..."

"Is it good?" He gasped and bit his lips.

"Uh-huh."

He extracted her panties in one move. "Oh, my," he said, eyes dilated over the delicate skin and the flow of honey. He bent down, licked her flesh with his tongue. She arched her spine, squeezed the bedsheets with her fists. Pleasure ran over her like water.

She came on his lips, trembling on his bed like a fish on a net.

He kissed her cheeks, eyes, lips. His palms pressed against her breasts. She removed her shirt and bra at once, revealing compact ripe breasts. He rolled his tongue around the caramel-colored nipples. A new wave of desire consumed her.

Vanessa reached for his groin, and he rolled to the side. She unzipped his shorts with urgency, a marvelous rigid sex popped up. The shape, the contours so perfect, as if sculpted by hand. His sex smelt of a neck in the early morning, sweaty from a damp sleep. It had the smoothest skin her lips ever touched. She licked languidly, in cat-like moves. His penis tasted like the sea. She inserted a small portion of it in her mouth and closed her lips around it. He quivered and let out a loud breath. She indulged herself, mouthful, filling the room with the noise of wet kisses. When he came, he held her head with both hands, caressing her scalp.

She rested on a pillow. Hair wild, eyes drugged. They exhaled in silence, facing each other, their breathing mixing. A grin fixed on their faces, the water of the canal singing in their ears.

"You're also handsome without glasses," she said, realizing that his glasses had been taken off.

"You think? And with glasses too?"

"Uh-huh. They give you so much charm. But without them, you're still sexy."

His lips broke into a wide smile. He slid his fingers around her neck. "It was the best I've ever had."

She chuckled. "You're kidding."

"I'm not. You suck me with so much passion. As if you want to eat it."

"I *do* want to eat it. It's delicious."

She took his hand and curled her tongue around his fingers. "It's smooth, beautiful. It's tasty."

He grabbed the violin curve of her waist. "You're getting me hard again."

She laughed. "Oh yeah? And if I say it has the most perfect size. It's so thick, it fills my whole mouth. It'll fit me perfectly." She jumped over his body, rubbed her vulva on him, her breasts grazing his eyes.

He kissed the plumpy nipples and said, "I don't have condoms, sweetheart. Is that a problem?"

She pouted, turning her butt in round movements. "How can you not have condoms?"

"I don't have a girlfriend, you know. And believe me, opportunities like this one are not common."

"You're so cute." She landed a kiss on his forehead, tossed down by his side. "How old are you?"

Hector's eyes dropped. "I'm afraid if I tell you, you won't come see me anymore."

Vanessa startled. "You're not telling me you're a minor, are you?"

"No." He giggled. "I'm 26."

"Oh, God. You are 10 years younger than me."

Hector drew her closer to his chest. "And so, what? Age is just a number."

"For how long have you had this boat, then? Since a child?"

"My grandpa gave me three years ago, as a graduation gift."

She ran her fingers around his torso. "What did you graduate in?"

"Graphic design. I wanted to study

philosophy but couldn't figure out what I would do with a philosophy degree."

"Your family is quite rich, then."

"Not really. My grandpa is an immigrant from Spain. He worked really hard throughout his life."

"Spain? My family also has a Spanish-speaking heritage. From Latin America, though."

His eyebrows lifted, "Latin America? That explains your beauty. You have the beautiful juicy buttocks of Latinas."

Vanessa smirked. "Have you looked at my ass?"

"Several times. Every time you passed by, I watched your ass ambling away, stretching the fabric of your clothes. What beautiful contours it has. I would stare at it and get aroused."

Vanessa playfully bit his upper arm.

"You're naughty."

"Yes, I am. And you are too." He rolled one hand down her hips, seizing the fulness of her butt cheeks.

"Uh-huh, that's right," said Vanessa, lifting her behind. "I'm so naughty that, before you come to bite my ass, I want another taste of you."

Vanessa drifted down his body. His hard sex quivered with her warm breath. The rosy head gleamed with moisture. She sucked in the silky skin and felt his flesh grow even harder and pulse.

Sensing eruption approaching, she pressed her breasts to his sex. He rubbed the head of his penis against her nipples, drawing circles. Within seconds her breasts were covered with creamy liquid dripping down.

The lights of the day had faded by the time they reached the entrance of her apartment. He had insisted on walking her home. They French kissed by the door and promised a whole night of pleasure for the weekend after. He would penetrate her and not take it off for hours. She would ride on him until her legs hurt.

She entered her apartment, her body exuding warmth. The fears she had left there in the early afternoon had dissipated. Uncertainty, disappointment, and loss were now dark clouds in a faraway sky.

Hector and Vanessa would meet every weekend when he wasn't working in his father's design company. The boat would bounce with their lovemaking. Fearing that passers-by could notice the vestiges of their wild performances, they sometimes made love in the woods. Under the fluffy flowers of a hawthorn tree, they exhausted their bodies with pleasure. He would caress her vulva with petals and hold the stalk of a flower in the mouth of her sex, while she sucked his penis until tiring her mouth.

She became obsessed with his sex. The caliber seemed to have been tailored around her proportions. It was as large enough to fill her completely yet not too long as to reach an uncomfortable depth.

"Oh, if I could borrow this delicious cock of yours and take it with me. I'd ride it all day and never stop."

When that bulky member inhabited her, pressing and rubbing and throbbing, inside her, it sent currents throughout her from head to toe... it consumed her body and inebriated her mind. It appeared to fulfil a missing part of her, a part that transported her to Eden.

About the Author

Andreia Rodrigues is a Brazilian author based in Europe. In addition to writing erotic stories, she has penned a memoir, a romance novel, and a collection of autobiographical essays. Her work is dedicated to inspiring readers to embrace their full potential, with a focus on well-crafted, female-centric erotic literature.

Other New Urge Titles You'll Enjoy

ANGEL OF EVERYTHING
Catherine D'Avis

PECULIAR CHARMS
Anonymous

THE SECRET OF GERANIUMS
Jessy Reine

THE RITES OF ECSTASY
Hélène Lavelle

HER THREE DAUGHTERS
Pierre Louÿs

HIDDEN GEMS
The Best of *The Pearl*
Various

THE NEW URGE READER OMNIBUS
Erotic Fiction by New Women Writers
Various

PETITES FOR TWO
Norman Conquest. ed.

VICTORIAN VICE: ANTHOLOGY OF FORBIDDEN PLEASURES
Lawrence Hamilton. ed.

Printed in Great Britain
by Amazon

45019579R00047